NO.1 BOY DETECTIVE

The Disappearing Daughter

Barbara Mitchelhill

Illustrated by
Tony Ross

ANDERSEN PRESS

For Emily, her librarian mum, Katy,
and her dad, Paul, who fixes my computer

This edition first published in 2017 by
Andersen Press Limited
20 Vauxhall Bridge Road
London SW1V 2SA
www.andersenpress.co.uk

First published by Andersen Press Limited in 2000

4 6 8 10 9 7 5 3

Text copyright © Barbara Mitchelhill, 2000
Illustrations copyright © Tony Ross, 2000

British Library Cataloguing in Publication Data available.

ISBN 978 1 78344 662 9

Printed and bound by Clays Ltd, St Ives Plc

Chapter 1

My name is Drooth. Damian Drooth. I track down criminals and solve crimes. A kind of one-kid, clean-up-the-world service.

How did I start? Let me tell you . . .

It was last year. The summer holidays had started and I was BORED! You know how it is when all your friends are away at the seaside or – worse still – at Disneyland.

I was riding on a 39 bus at the time.
I was feeling dead miserable, when I
noticed a book on the seat next to me.
A Hundred Ways to Catch a Criminal. I
had nothing better to do – so I read it.

After that I was hooked! My life
changed overnight. I was no longer a
bored brat. A droopy drop-out. I was a
supersleuth and my mission was to rid
the world of crime.

As it turned out, I didn't have long to wait. I was in the supermarket that afternoon. I was heading for the Assorted Crisps Section, when I saw a man lurking behind the freezers. Suspicious! I thought. A villain if ever I saw one! If I was going to prevent a crime, I had to act fast. So I jumped on the vegetable counter and shouted, 'THIEF! OVER THERE! GET HIM!'

For a second, everybody in the supermarket stood still and stared at me. Then they rushed over to the Freezer Section. (The crook was shaking with fear by this time.) They surrounded him. Some bashed him

with their shopping baskets. Others grabbed him. He was finished, I could tell.

Me? I stayed cool and walked through the checkout. I didn't want publicity.

But that day, there was more . . .

On the way home, I saw a man
snatch a bag outside a shop. He slung
it into a big black Rover and drove off.
A getaway car! I knew about them. I
pulled out my supersleuth notebook
and scribbled down the registration
number. Then I dashed down the
street to find a telephone.

'Excuse me!' I said to the woman in the call box. 'This is an emergency.' I grabbed the phone and dialled 999.

That was my first day as a crime buster. Pretty good, eh?

Unfortunately, Mum didn't see it that way. On Friday, she got two letters.

Dear Madam,

Please do us a favour and keep your son out of our supermarket. My store detective does not like being accused of shoplifting by a small boy. He was very embarrassed. He was only doing his job.

Yours faithfully,

P J Handy

Manager, Save-a-Lot Superstore

Dear Mrs Drooth,

No thanks to your son, I almost spent last night in jail. Please explain to him that I was putting an old lady's shopping bag into my taxi. I was not snatching it. He must be barmy to think that.

A L Fair
Ace Taxi Company

When Mum read the letters, her face turned a weird shade of purple. This happens when she gets angry (which is quite often lately). I think she should go and see a doctor.

13

Chapter 2

I have to admit, I made mistakes at first. So I started studying dead seriously. I wanted to be the best private eye ever. I watched loads of films on TV. I sat in my pyjamas in the front room with the curtains drawn. All day long. Black and white films. Colour films. Films about Sherlock Holmes . . . Miss Marple . . . Mike Hammer . . . Inspector Morse . . . You name 'em – I watched 'em.

Mum wasn't impressed. 'It's sunny outside,' she said. 'Why don't you play football like the other kids? It's not natural.'

15

It's difficult to be a supersleuth in our street. But I was determined! By the end of the week I had watched so many crimes being solved that I worked out a theory of my own!

This is my theory.

ANYONE WITH EYES SET CLOSE TOGETHER IS NOT TO BE TRUSTED AND IS UP TO NO GOOD. THEY ARE VERY PROBABLY CRIMINALS.

After that, I knew I was ready to start my career. I would go out and track down crooks . . . swindlers . . . bank robbers . . . forgers (I must remember to check my piggy bank for counterfeit coins). It was a serious task. I decided to start the next day.

Just my luck! Mum saw me slipping out of the back door in my supersleuth gear. She looked at me suspiciously. 'Just going to solve a crime, Mum,' I explained but she slammed the door shut. 'No way, Damian,' she said. 'I

want to keep my eye on you. You can
forget this detective stuff. I don't want
more embarrassing letters.'

This was bad news. Did James Bond
ever have problems like this? Was
Sherlock Holmes ever kept in by his
mum? No! I felt depressed.

'You can come to work with me,' said Mum. 'That will keep you out of trouble.'

Mum runs a company called HOME COOKING UNLIMITED. She cooks for weddings and parties and stuff like that. When she takes me with her, I always get stuck with the washing up. Dead boring.

'I'm up at Harbury Hall today,' she said as we packed the van with a million bread rolls. 'There's a film crew working up there all week.'

A film crew, eh? Actors. Camera
operators. Stunt artists. I began to feel
quite perky.

'Don't get any funny ideas,' said
Mum. 'You're doing the washing up.'

What did I tell you?

Once we were on the site, Mum
carried piles of plates into the food
tent. (I am never allowed to do this
after a little accident I had last year.
Can I help it if plates are slippery?)

I sat and ate my early morning bag of crisps and read the newspaper. (We detectives have to keep up-to-date.) It was *full* of stories of unsolved crimes. The police clearly needed help. And here I was trapped in a food tent. What a waste of a brilliant mind!

But things brightened up later. A man called Victor DeVito dropped into the tent. As it turned out, he was the film director. A real big shot! He didn't go anywhere without a crowd of people taking notes and saying, 'Yes, Victor.' 'Just as you say, Victor.'

I had never met a film director before. But I stayed cool. I kept my

autograph book in my pocket. I'd wait till later.

'Howdee, ma'am!' he said to my mum. (He was American.) 'I just stopped by to introduce myself. You catering folk are real important on the set. Yes, sir!'

I could tell Mum was pleased. She gave one of those funny smiles and her cheeks turned pink.

'And who are you, sonny?' he said to me.

'Damian Drooth, Supersleuth,' I said. Then I whipped out the Identity Card I'd made the night before. He was dead impressed.

'Well, Damian! I can tell you that there are plenty of crooks in the film business. Watch out for 'em, will you?'

My first commission! A crime watcher on a film set. Wow! I couldn't promise to catch *every* crook but I'd do my best. From now on, I'd be on the lookout.

Chapter 3

Mr DeVito had a daughter called Trixibelle. An unusual name, you must admit. But everybody's got to be called something.

You could tell her dad was rich. She had all the gear. The trainers. The flash jacket. The personal stereo. But she was OK. She stayed behind when her dad went to check out cameras and stuff. She gave me a packet of Charley Chip's Chocolate Drops. She had loads. Personally, I prefer Smoky Bacon Crisps.

'You're so lucky, Damian,' she said as we sat eating. 'You've got a mom who cooks for you. My mom's just an actress, you know. She's never home. Right now she's in Hong Kong.'

'Acting's really interesting,' I said. But Trixibelle shook her head.

'It's not as interesting as cooking. That's what I want to do when I grow up. But Pops says I'll be too rich to be a cook.'

Being rich sounded pretty good to me. At least you didn't get stuck with the washing up.

Somebody was calling her name outside the tent.

'That'll be my new tutor, Miss Berry,' she sighed. 'I'll have to go.'

I was amazed. I'd never met anyone with a personal tutor. But then I'd never met anyone as rich as the DeVito family.

Trixibelle walked away from the tent. Her tutor was waiting by the large white caravan opposite. Wow!

Was that really a teacher? She looked like a film star! She was tall with long blonde hair and red lipstick. And she wore really cool shades, too. She was nothing like Mr Grimethorpe, our class teacher. Lucky old Trixibelle!

By half past ten there was a long queue outside the food tent. Hungry actors. Ravenous technicians. All wanting Mum's coffee and cakes. Me? I was soon up to my elbows in greasy water. I ask you! After an hour and a half, my hands had turned ghostly white and as wrinkled as prunes.

'If you can't do it faster than that, Damian, we'll never be ready for lunch,' Mum moaned.

I admit I wasn't the fastest washer-up in the world. It was hard keeping my mind on dirty plates. Luckily, I was saved from total boredom when one of the security guards stuck his head into the tent.

'Anybody seen Trixibelle?' he asked.

I lifted my hands out of the water. 'She's in the caravan over there,' I said, pointing across the grass.

The guard shook his head. 'Not for half an hour,' he said. 'Her tutor reported her missing. Miss Berry went out to get a cup of coffee and when she got back, Trixibelle had gone.'

'I'll find her,' I said, drying my hands on a tea towel. 'I'm brilliant at tracking down missing persons.' This was not strictly true. But it was a great excuse to get away from the washing up.

Mum wasn't keen. Her lips were pressed tight together. 'He's got work to do,' she said.

The guard looked daggers. 'Mr DeVito will be very angry if we lose his daughter,' he said in a threatening kind of way. 'Your son would be a great help.'

So Mum let me go.

That was how the Case of the Disappearing Daughter began.

Chapter 4

I wasn't really worried about Trixibelle. In my opinion, she had slipped off somewhere to get away from lessons. I knew all about that. I'd done it myself. Particularly during spelling tests.

I followed the guard across the grass. Miss Berry was standing by the caravan. She had a large tissue clasped to her nose and she was sniffing. I could tell she was upset.

'Try not to worry, Miss Berry,' I
said. 'I'll get her back for you. You can
rely on me.'

She gave me a wonderful smile and
a tingle ran from the top of my head
down to my toes. I felt like a knight on
a crusade.

It seemed that everyone was out searching for Trixibelle. (Except Mum who was doing the washing up.) The whole crew had stopped work to look. I used all my detective's experience – but still I found nothing. Not a single clue.

Suddenly, Victor DeVito came rushing out of his caravan (the biggest on the site) and climbed onto the roof. Was the man crazy or what?

'Listen, people!' he shouted through his megaphone.

Everything went deathly quiet.

'I have some terrible news.
My Trixibelle has been kidnapped!'

There were gasps of oohs and aaahs.
Nobody could believe it.

'It's true!' the director continued,
holding his hand up for silence. (Mr
Grimethorpe, our class teacher, often
does this.) 'I just got a phone call and
some crazy people are demanding a
million pounds for my baby.'

He took a large handkerchief and
blew his nose.

'I'll pay it if I have to – but in the meantime, the police are doing their best to find out where she is.'

Now I know for a fact that the police often miss clues that are right under their noses. So I decided that somehow, I would have to track down the criminals. After all, Victor DeVito himself had asked me to be on the lookout for crooks. It was the least I could do.

Chapter 5

I hurried back to tell Mum about the kidnapping.

'I've heard,' she said. 'Miss Berry is very upset. She's gone to lie down.'

Poor Miss Berry! I thought. She must be feeling dead guilty. Letting Mr DeVito's daughter slip away.

'I think I'll take her a cup of tea,' I said. 'She'll like that.' This was a good chance to impress Miss Berry with my supersleuth ideas for finding Trixibelle.

'That's thoughtful of you, Damian,' said Mum. I could tell she was surprised.

I was careful not to spill the tea as I pushed open the caravan door. I suppose I should have knocked – but I didn't. What I saw shocked me, I can tell you. Miss Berry wasn't lying down at all. She was bending over, stuffing clothes into a suitcase.

I scanned the caravan with my detective laser vision. On a table were a pair of shades and a long blonde wig. I gasped. That was when Miss Berry whizzed round. What a shock! She wasn't blonde after all. She had short dark hair.

'Oh dear!' she said, grabbing hold of
her wig. 'What a mess I look, Damian!
I . . . I was just keeping myself busy.
Just tidying up.' She slammed the
suitcase shut and took the cup and
saucer. 'How very kind of you, dear
boy. Poor, poor Trixibelle.'

She smiled but she couldn't win me
over. Things had changed. Now I
could see that her eyes were set very
close together. If my theory was right,
Miss Berry was a criminal in disguise.

Chapter 6

After that, I decided to keep an eye on the caravan. This was difficult as Mum insisted I finished the washing up. I had to keep looking over my shoulder. My neck got terrible cramp. It was agony.

Nothing happened for a bit. Then
Mum asked me to take the rubbish
out. What a piece of luck! Just as I left
the tent, I saw Miss Berry sneaking out
of the caravan. She was carrying a
suitcase! I dumped the rubbish sack
and followed her – keeping my
distance just like detectives do.

Before long, I realised that she was
heading for the car park. So she had a
car! She could be away in no time.
Then my prime suspect would be lost
for ever.

She stopped by a large red Ford and
took some keys from her handbag. I
dropped down between two vans and

watched over the bonnet. My heart
was pounding like a rock band. She
was going to escape. How could I stop
her?

As she opened the door, a voice
shouted, 'Hey you! Wait!'

Miss Berry spun round. A security
guard was hurrying towards her.

'You're not thinking of leaving the
site, are you, miss?'

Her piggy eyes nearly popped out of
her head. I could see she was shaking.

'Just going for a little ride,' she said,
cool as you like.

'Mr DeVito said *nobody* should leave,' said the guard who was pretty scary.

But Miss Berry smiled and walked round the car. 'I'm so upset, officer. Trixibelle is my dear little pupil, you see.' You could tell the guard was taken in by her film star looks. She stood there telling him loads of lies. And he believed her! It was clear he wasn't well trained in detective work.

I didn't waste any time. While they were talking on one side of the car, I crept around the other side. Slowly, I opened the back door. I slipped in and I lay on the floor behind the driver's seat. Wherever Miss Berry was going, so was I!

Chapter 7

Miss Berry drove like a maniac. She whizzed round bends. She tore down hills. I felt sick, I can tell you. When I heard her dialling on the car phone, I couldn't believe it! It was crazy! She couldn't drive with two hands – never mind one!

'Zac! It's me,' she said. 'I'm on my way. Are you ready to move the girl? DeVito should come up with the money within the next hour.'

So my theory of close-set eyes was right. Miss Berry was a criminal. A kidnapper, no less! I was on her track. All I had to do was to get Trixibelle out of her clutches.

When she screeched to a halt, my head smashed against the back of the seat. SPLAT! I lay there. My brain was spinning. I heard the car door open then Miss Berry walked away. Somehow, I had to get up!

I was seeing stars but I pulled myself together. I peeped out of the window. We had stopped in a deserted farmyard – but there was no sign of Miss Berry. Just loads of barns and derelict sheds. It was a perfect hiding place. Nobody would come to a place like this.

The problem was – where to start looking. Trixibelle could be anywhere.

I opened the car door and slid onto the ground. Like a marine on a combat mission, I crabbed my way across the farmyard. Except for the noise of swallows twittering, there wasn't a sound. No voice. Nothing.

I stood up. I pressed my back to the wall and hoped Miss Berry wasn't looking out of one of the windows. My forehead was sticky with sweat (or was it blood?)

I raced across to a large barn. I stopped and stood panting by a doorway. That was when my luck changed. I glanced down and saw a trail of chocolate drops. They were Charley Chip's Chocolate Drops. I could spot them a mile off. Trixibelle had left a clue! Good thinking!

I felt hopeful. I walked through the door of the barn and climbed some stone steps. It was dark inside and I had to feel my way. Luckily, the chocolate drops went right to the top.

They led to a wooden door and I pressed my ear against it. Voices! That guy called Zac and Miss Berry!

I panicked. Well, who wouldn't? I needed help. I had to run.

I was about to turn and go back when the worst thing possible happened. The door opened.

'You!' said Miss Berry.

'Who's he?' yelled the man. (This was Zac.)

Miss Berry leaned forward to grab me.

I stepped backward.

Miss Berry slipped.

Zac tripped over her.

Smash! They crashed down the stairs. Bang! Clunk! Boing!

They even pulled some bales of hay on top of them. There they lay, moaning. Only their feet and arms visible. What a sight!

Trixibelle was in the room upstairs, bound and gagged. No problem! I had

her free in a flash.

'You're wonderful, Damian,' she said. She flung her arms round my neck and gave me a sloppy kiss.

I was dead embarrassed. 'Don't mention it,' I said. 'It was nothing.'

We raced downstairs where the two kidnappers were lying moaning under the bales. Their arms were flailing about – but they couldn't move.

'Sit on 'em,' I said. 'That way they can't get away.'

Trixi sat on her tutor. I sat on Zac. The problem was, what to do next? If one of us went for help, one of the kidnappers could get free. But we couldn't stay here for ever. My brain

was pounding, trying to find a
solution. What would Sherlock Holmes
do? What would James Bond do? What
would Superman do?

'We could always use my mobile,'
said Trixibelle.

I was gobsmacked! She fished a
phone out of her pocket and dialled
999. She was smarter than I thought.

Chapter 8

In no time the barn was surrounded.
Five police cars – not to mention the
Range Rovers bringing Victor DeVito
and the entire film crew.

'We're here, babe!' shouted Mr
DeVito through his megaphone. 'Your
daddy's come to get you.'

Miss Berry and Zac were soon locked up in a police cell. We went back to Harbury Hall and Victor DeVito threw a fantastic party. There was mountains of food and I didn't have to wash up.

'I'm proud of you, Damian,' said Trixi's dad.

My mum nodded and wiped a tear from her eye.

'You saved my baby, sonny,' said Victor. 'Thank you sincerely.'

It was all a bit embarrassing. 'It's the training that does it,' I explained. 'I'm a well-known supersleuth in my home town. It was all in a day's work.'

Victor nodded as if he understood. I could tell he was dead impressed.

Afterwards the police inspector came to talk to me. I think he wanted to pick up some tips on solving crimes.

'A real detective looks for clues,' I said.

He pulled his notebook out ready to

jot down my ideas.

'And what clues made you suspect these two?'

I smiled. 'It's all a question of experience,' I said. I didn't mention my theory of close-set eyes. That's my little secret! They don't call me Supersleuth for nothing.